MO[NA]
the VAMPIRE

The Big Brown Bap Monster

CINAR

Television series © 1999 Fancy Cape Productions Inc.
a subsidiary of CINAR Corporation/Alphanim, France
3, Canal J. All rights reserved.

ORCHARD BOOKS
96 Leonard Street, London EC2A 4XD
Orchard Books Australia
32/45-51 Huntley Street, Alexandria, NSW 2015
ISBN 1 84362 815 5
First published in Great Britain in 1996
This edition published in 2004
Text © Hiawyn Oram 1996
Illustrations © Sonia Holleyman 1996
The rights of Hiawyn Oram to be identified as the author and
of Sonia Holleyman to be identified as the illustrator of this work
have been asserted by them in accordance with the
Copyright, Designs and Patents Act, 1988.
A CIP catalogue record for this book is available from the British Library.
1 3 5 7 9 10 8 6 4 2
Printed in Great Britain

MONA
the VAMPIRE
The Big Brown Bap Monster

HIAWYN ORAM

Illustrated by
SONIA HOLLEYMAN

ORCHARD BOOKS

CONTENTS

1. Through Half-closed Eyes 11

2. No Vampires Tonight 15

3. An Unexpected Turn 19

4. A Princess Giant Joins in 24

5. In the Bap Lair 28

6. Swallowed Whole 32

7. The Big Crash 40

8. Escape from the Planet Zogg 44

9. Scared to Bits 50

10. Firm Friends and Another
    Transformation 58

COLUMBUS CLOSE OFF OLD STREET

CABOT CANAL

ALLOTMENTS

RALEIGH

DA GAMA

3 NAPPS' OLD HOUSE

CHARLEY KNEES' HOUSE

COLUMBUS DRIVE

CHENGHO ST.

MONAS' HOUSE

CORTES ST.

THE CAST

MONA

SPIDER

FANG

GOLDEN

LILY

Chapter 1
Through Half-closed Eyes

Mona and Fang were in the kitchen having Tuesday tea: vegebangers in big, brown, wholemeal baps for Mona and nothing for Fang if Mona's mother was watching.

Luckily, this Tuesday she wasn't watching. She was getting the dining room ready for her Healers meeting.

11

"Oh, and Mona," she called, "there's a little girl called Lily coming tonight. Her parents have moved in round the corner and she's your age and she'll be going to St Faith's so I thought it'd be nice if you made friends first."

"OK," said Mona, slipping Fang another banger. "Me and Fang were just looking forward to a really nice game with someone, weren't we Fang?"

crunch!
munch!
slurp!

Mmm said Fang, his mouth too full to speak.

Mona stared round the kitchen with new interest. If there was going to be someone her age to play with, she'd better think of something someone her age would want to play.

And then, suddenly, there it was. When she half-closed her eyes, the last brown bap on the counter was no longer the last brown bap on the counter. It had seedy eyes and huge blubbery lips and was billowing and puffing and getting bigger by the second.

"Will you look at that!" Mona leapt on to a chair.

Fang obediently arched his back.

"It's the Big Brown Bap Monster!" Mona muffled. "Don't scream, Fang, don't yell your head off with screechy scaredness…

Chapter 2
No Vampires Tonight

It was dark and dusty under Mona's bed. But at least it was safe from Big Brown Bap Monsters – for the moment. It was also where Mona kept her box of vampire things.

"Now," said Mona as Fang coughed and sneezed through the dust. "I suppose you're saying the only thing that can scare away Bap Monsters is vampires."

Fang sneezed a definite yes.

"Then vampires it will have to be," said Mona, wriggling out from under the bed with the box and emptying the contents all over her duvet. However, before she'd even stuck in her glow-in-the-dark fangs, her mother was at the door.

"Lily's here," she said.

"OK," said Mona, grabbing her dressing gown to use for a terrifying cape. "I'll be down in a minute."

"No," said her mother, removing the cape. "You'll be down now. And not as a vampire."

Mona began to explain about vampires being the only things that could scare away Bap Monsters. But her mother wouldn't hear. "Mona," she said, in her Gentle-But-Absolutely-Firm voice. "This is my Healers evening. Mrs Duncan hasn't been here before. Lily hasn't met you before and it's this simple: no vampires tonight."

So Mona and Fang had to go downstairs not as vampires.

"Well, don't blame me if we're gobbled," Mona warned, peering through the banisters to get her first glimpse of Lily.

Chapter 3
An Unexpected Turn

Immediately, at first glimpse, her heart sank. And with each step down the stairs it sank further. Lily was clearly no Bap Scarer. Most of her was hidden behind her mother's skirt but what could be seen was trembly and delicate, her huge eyes brimming with fright.

Mrs Duncan prised Lily's fingers from her skirt as Mona's mother did the introductions.

"She's very shy," Mrs Duncan apologised. Mona's mother clucked sympathetically, opening the sitting room door. "Well, I tell you what. Why don't they go in here. My husband's in here. He'll keep an eye on them and they can play Animal Pairs or something till we're finished."

So, under her father's watchful eye from behind his newspaper, Mona got out the Animal Pairs, the Gigglywinks and the Junior Monopoly – doing her very best not to show she'd rather be upstairs preparing to meet the Bap Monster.

"OK, which one?" said Mona.

She patiently named each game.

Lily shook her head at each.

Mona offered headstands in the corner armchair.

Lily shook her head.

Mona offered TV or one of her mother's Polish-Up-Your-Karate videos.

Shy Lily hung her head →

Lily shook her head.

Mona's father offered Blind Man's Bluff, I Spy with My Little Eye and Poker as a joke.

Lily shook her head.

Fang offered himself for stroking.

But still Lily shook her head.

Mona sighed inwardly, realising that unless she was very careful she and Fang were doomed to an evening of nothing. She looked over to check her father had retired behind his newspaper and then had one, last, desperate try.

"OK," she whispered, "do you want to come upstairs and see my vampire things...?"

For a second everything in the room, even breathing, froze. Then, to Mona and Fang's amazement, Lily raised her huge blue eyes and ever so slightly nodded.

Brown Baps Beware!

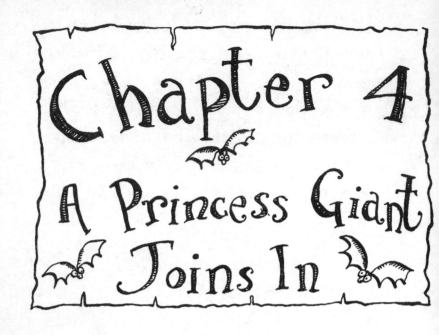

Chapter 4
A Princess Giant Joins In

Lily stared but said nothing while Mona and Fang put on their vampire things, the better to show them to her.

But when Mona explained that she didn't have any more vampire things for Lily to put on, and Bap Monsters could only be scared away by vampires, she did speak—and not that faintly either…

There must be something else.....

"Fang says giants," said Mona crayoning in her vampire eyes.

"Giants?" said Lily, nervous again.

Big, big giants coughed Fang.

"No, no," said Mona. "Not big giants. Just ordinary giants."

Immediately Lily brightened.

"I could be a Princess Giant. In your mother's high heels," she ventured.

Mona leapt up. "OK, wait here," she said and ran to her mother's room and back before Lily could change her mind.

"My mother's a karate expert so she doesn't have high heels," she panted.

"But I brought you low high heels and necklaces and lipstick and you can use my duvet cover for your train ... and ... and ..." she pulled the cover off the duvet and picked up her stuffed lion, "you can have Golden for your faithful servant ..."

"All right," said Lily, letting Mona and Fang help turn her into a Princess Giant in not much more than a trice. Then, with Mona announcing them the famous Most Frightening Bap Scarers, they slithered down the stairs and across the hall on their tummies so

26

the Bap Monster wouldn't hear them coming.

And just when it was least expecting it, they jumped up and burst into its lair, yelling...

Chapter 5
In the Bap Lair

"Flour-freeze you mean. Baps don't have blood." Mona's father was sitting in the Bap Lair, eating a cheese bap, unaware of the danger he was in.

"Well, this one does!" cried Mona. "And you'd better watch out because its right behind you. On the fridge, full of gnashing teeth and the size of a flying saucer!"

"Oh no, oh help, oh where?" Mona's father ducked down in terror.

"You can't see it because you're grown up, but don't worry, it's there, isn't it Lily?" Lily nodded, her huge eyes seeing it as large as life.

"Then I'd better get out of here before it gobbles me invisibly!" said Mona's father, grabbing his bap and dashing for the Lair door. "Just make sure you take care of Her Royal Highness, the Princess Lily!"

As soon as her father had disappeared, Mona drew the curtains so her glow-in-the-dark fangs would glow better.

She lifted up her arms so her cape and her elasticated spiders would cast terrifying shadows on the walls.

RRRRRRRRGH
SCAT BAP MONSTER BACK
WHERE YOU CAME FROM !

Then paling noticeably, she rummaged in a drawer for some wooden spoons and dived under the table.

"Quick everyone! Get into the cave! It isn't dark enough. The Bap Monster isn't scared. It isn't scared at all. It's just whirr-blobbing towards us. It's smacking its two-slice lips. It's gnashing its seedy teeth. Here, Princess Giant, here Vampire Cat, take these magic swords and swash them round or ... PREPARE TO BE EATEN ALIVE!"

Chapter 6
Swallowed Whole

"Are we eaten yet?" breathed Lily.

"Not yet!" cried Mona. "So keep on swashing and swashing."

The three of them swashed wildly from the safety of the cave. But it was no good.

"Oh no!" cried Mona. "It isn't bothered by swords. Look, it's eaten Fang's. And now it's eating mine!"

"What'll we do?" whispered Lily.

"Don't worry, you've still got yours," said Mona. "And your magic necklaces. Use your magic necklaces to turn your sword into a magic wand. Then with your magic wand turn Golden into a Magic Genie …"

"Now ask Golden to save us," said Mona. "Say, 'Golden Genie, Golden Genie, faithful Golden Genie, turn the Big Brown Bap Monster into a mouse so Fang can pounce!'"

Lily hesitated.

"Go on," Mona yelled. "Hurry!"

Still Lily hesitated.

You do it! hissed Fang.

Mona grabbed Golden and crawled to the mouth of the cave. But when she crawled back, she had only bad news.

"The Bap Monster wasn't afraid of Golden either. It just went, 'Yummy, yummy, a lovely fat Golden Genie' and gobbled him up. And now it's whirr-blobbing right into our cave going,

'Yummy, yummy, a lovely fat Vampire Cat and a lovely fat Princess Giant'. It's swallowing you, Fang. It's swallowing you, Lily. And now, oh whoops, oh dear, oh help, oh help … IT'S EVEN SWALLOWED … ME!"

"OK in there?" Mona's father put his head round the Bap Lair door.

"Fine!" said Mona. "The Bap Monster's swallowed us. That's all."

Whole mewed Fang.

"Like Jonah in the whale," said Mona's father.

"Like three Jonahs in a Bap," said Mona.

"Four with Golden," said Lily, clasping Golden tightly.

"Well, you'll have to dance on its ribs for forty days and forty nights till it can't bear any more and spits you out," said Mona's father.

"Oh yes!" breathed Lily.

"Not yet!" snapped Mona, wriggling out from under the table and whirling round in circles. "Because don't you know, right now, the Bap Monster's whirr-whizzing us through space. And we don't want to be spitted out in the middle of space, do we?"

"Not without oxygen masks," said Mona's father. "Well, I'll be in the Sitting Room Galaxy if you need me. And good luck!"

"Come on you two!" Mona was whirling round so hard she was already giddy. "The Bap Monster's whirr-spinning us into the Hall Galaxy..."

Fang and Lily scrambled to join Mona in the dark nearly-empty beauty of Hall Galaxy.

"And now it's making for the Sitting Room Galaxy!" cried Mona. "It's in the Sitting Room Galaxy! And it's going so fast it's nearly crashing...."

Chapter 7
The Big Crash

"Into my meteor…" said a booming voice…

My sofa-shaped meteor, home of me, the Lonely Meteor Giant

"Well, don't worry, we're not stopping, Meteor Giant. We're on our way…to the Garden Galaxy!" cried Mona.

"This is my favourite," breathed Lily as they whirled around in the starry darkness.

Me too, hissed Fang.

"No, no!" cried Mona. "Don't you know anything? This is the most dangerous galaxy. It's full of Black Holes. If we're not careful, the Bap Monster will be sucked into a black hole with us inside it...and that'll be the end of everything...we'll never get out..."

"Then we'll have to turn back," shivered Lily, suddenly seeing Black Holes everywhere.

So they all rattled and yelled until they had the Bap Monster whirr-whizzing back through the Sitting Room Galaxy into the safety of the Hall Galaxy.

Only by that time they were so giddy from spinning and whirling, they were completely out of control and could not stop.

And the next thing any of them knew, they'd whirr-whizzed where they shouldn't — and crash-landed in a terrible screeching jangle and tangle of arms and legs...right in the middle of Mona's mother's Meeting.

Chapter 8

Escape from the Planet Zogg

Now we're in for it, spluttered Fang.

Six pairs of Healers' eyes stared down at them. Four looked very disturbed. One looked very, very cross. One rolled in shock.

"Mona!" said the Cross-Eyes (Mona's mother's). "What do you think you're doing?" But before Mona could even start to answer, something completely unexpected happened. Lily stood up – without a tremble or a blush – and picked up Golden. She straightened her train calmly and put on a missing low high heel.

Then she spoke - or rather she erupted in a flow of words - as if she'd been holding back all her life and didn't need to hold back anymore.

Lily the Princess Giant speaks out ← out

"We are the famous Monster Bap Scarers ... at your service." She bowed low. "I am Lily the Princess Giant. This is Golden my faithful Magic Genie. This is Mona the Vampire, Chief Scarer of Monsters, and Other Things That Go Creak In the Night and this is Fang, her assistant."

The pair of shocked, rolling eyes - Lily's mother's - looked as if they were

Mrs Duncan

going to roll right out of her head. But this didn't stop Lily.

"We were swallowed by the Big Brown Bap Monster, like Jonahs, and whirred through many galaxies," she continued as easily as Fang might purr. "But now we're spitted out here... on..." she stifled a giggle, "... the great Planet Zogg."

She bowed low again but mainly because she was doubled up with giggles.

When the fit passed she pointed over to Mona's bike propped up in a corner. "And, oh look, a space capsule awaits us. If you, the great Zoggians, will allow the Chief Bap Scarer to get to it, we'll be gone in a flash and trouble you no more..."

Mona, her mouth open, looked over at her mother. Her mother, with her mouth open, gave a small nod and

Mona ran over to the bike. She jumped on, circled the table at great speed to show off her space-bike capsule skills, stopped to pick up the others – and fled.

Chapter 9
Scared To Bits

Mona was pedalling so hard that once back in the hall, they almost had a very nasty crash. Luckily her father was there to catch the bike and steady them.

"Hmmm," he said. "I expect your mother's very cross - having her meeting interrupted."

"Well, she was," said Mona, dismounting. "But then Lily explained."

"Lily explained?" said Mona's father.

Yes, and she's a guest so it was all right

"Even so," said her father, "if I were you, I'd end this adventure now."

"Oh but we can't," cried Lily, jumping up and down. "Because the Bap Monster spitted us out but it's not got rid of yet."

"You're right!" cried Mona running to check the kitchen. "It's back on the fridge puffing and gnashing its teeth."

Well, when ARE you going to get rid of it? hissed Fang. *'Cos I'm famished.*

"What about Bap Bait?" said Lily. "We could lure it back into the bap bag with bait and then throw it in the bin!"

Brilliant said Fang. *Cheese would do it.*

"Brilliant," said Mona's father, retiring to the sitting room. "And then that must be that."

"Not brilliant one bit!" said Mona, wanting Lily to join in properly but not wanting her to have all the good ideas. "It might burst out and eat the bin men. But we could lure it into the hall here and scare it to bits. And I know how!"

She raced upstairs to the bathroom re-appearing a few moments later with her big, yellow, foot-shaped sponge, dripping and squelching wet.

Then she ran down the stairs and switched off the overhead light, leaving on the table lamps. And this time when she raised her arms, her cape made such terrifying shadows and her spiders jiggled so horrifyingly she knew nothing would go wrong now.

"See, here it comes. Out of the kitchen, whirr-blobbling over to the bait..." Mona called through bared fangs. "And this time it IS frightened enough!"

RRRRRRAAARGH! BEWARE OF LILY THE PRINCESS GIANT WITH HER MAGIC GENIE THAT CAN TURN ANYTHING INTO ANYTHING.....

Then DO it hissed Fang from under the coat stand.

"WE ARE!" cried Mona. "WE ARE! AND NOW IT'S SO FRIGHTENED IT'S GOING TO EXPLODE. IN FACT IT IS EXPLODING! INTO A MILLION BITS. A MILLION TRILLION BITS. IT'S EXPLODING INTO SO MANY BITS. IT'S EXPLODING INTO AIR! THERE! BANG! IT'S EXPLODED!"

Chapter 10
Firm Friends And Another Transformation

Mona snapped the light back on.

"WOW!" said Lily, "That was AMAZING!"

Can we get something to eat now? mewed Fang.

"OK," said Mona. "Peanut butter biscuits as they're your favourite!" But before they could get to the kitchen,

Mona's mother and Mrs Duncan emerged from the dining room.

"Mona, Lily has to go home now."

"I'm afraid we do," said Mrs Duncan.

"Ohhhhh," Lily groaned. "Just a bit longer. I'm having the best time ever."

"Sorry," said Mrs Duncan, taking off Lily's train. "But I must say what's happened here tonight is incredible. Why, Lily is...well, she's completely transformed!"

"Does that mean she can come and play tomorrow?" said Mona. "Because after Angela she can be my best friend now. And she can borrow Golden if she likes."

"Well, that's very kind and we'll see about tomorrow..." Mrs Duncan sounded a bit flustered. But she did kiss Mona's mother - which seemed a good sign - before ushering Lily, clasping Golden, down the garden path.

And while Mona's mother said goodbye to the other Healers, Mona and Fang went to check out a few things with her father.

"What exactly does transformed mean?" she said taking out her fangs and cuddling up.

"Changed from one thing to another," said her father. "Usually something better."

"Then Mum won't be cross that Lily got transformed in our house?"

"She should be very pleased," said Mona's father. "And very proud of you as you helped it come about."

"Well, it was our game that did it," said Mona. "You see, Dad, it was only a game. There wasn't really a Bap Monster."

Not an actual one, purred Fang.

"Oh yes," said her father. "In that case would you mind telling me where all the peanut butter biscuits have gone?"

Prob'ly just transformed yawned Fang.

And Mona didn't argue. She'd already entered Dream Galaxy and didn't even hear the question.

MONA the VAMPIRE

HIAWYN ORAM * SONIA HOLLEYMAN

COLLECT ALL THE FANGTASTIC MONA THE VAMPIRE STORIES:

MONA the VAMPIRE   The Hairy Hands   1 84362 816 3

MONA the VAMPIRE   The Big Brown Bap Monster   1 84362 815 5

MONA the VAMPIRE   The Tinned Poltergeist   1 84362 814 7

MONA the VAMPIRE   The Jackpot Disaster   1 84362 817 1

 All priced at £3.99

Mona the Vampire titles are available from all good book shops, or can be ordered
direct from the publisher: Orchard Books, PO BOX 29, Douglas IM99 1BQ
Credit card orders please telephone 01624 836000
or fax 01624 837033 or visit our Internet site: www.wattspub.co.uk
or e-mail: bookshop@enterprise.net for details.

To order please quote title, author and ISBN and your full name and address.
Cheques and postal orders should be made payable to 'Bookpost plc.'
Postage and packing is FREE within the UK
(overseas customers should add £1.00 per book).
Prices and availability are subject to change.